SONGS OF FAITH

SONGS

OF FAITH

◄O►

Angela Johnson

SCHOLASTIC INC.
New York Toronto London Auckland Sydney
Mexico City New Delhi Hong Kong

ISBN 0-439-16398-6

12 11 10 9 8 7 6 5 4 3 2 1   0 1 2 3 4 5/0

Printed in the U.S.A.   40

First Scholastic printing, February 2000

Book design by Mina Greenstein
The text of this book is set in 12.5 New Baskerville.

TO DOMINIC

SONGS OF FAITH

ONE
◂◦▸

I jump down from the ledge of the building and it's like flying. I used to tell Daddy I'd fly when I got older and he'd smile. It just came to me he thought I meant become a pilot, and I feel like any understanding we ever had for each other was eaten away in a blink.

I walk on toward home and hide my paint-brush inside a garbage can, in front of the pawn-shop that's been doing pretty good since the mills have started closing. All the buildings look taller in the dead of night.

Chicago might look like this. Daddy's there.

He's there and I'm here. If he's thinking about me, it probably isn't about me prowling Harvey, Ohio, with a paintbrush thinking about him.

"CALL ME ROBERT from now on, okay, Doreen?"

It's five o'clock in the morning and my brother's kneeling by my bed shining his flashlight in my face. At 5 A.M. I can't move my mouth to say "Bobo," which has always been his name to me, 'cause I've just sneaked in from painting big yellow smiling faces on all the Bicentennial signs that the city has hung up near the projects. It's still 1975, and I don't think the country is going to be too upset if Harvey has only two million things painted red, white, and blue instead of two million and fifty.

Can't really deal with my brother just now. So I turn over and grunt into my pillow, then he leaves. Before I doze off again I think I'll ask him at breakfast what he's talking about.

MAMA DOT is somewhere in the house typing. Maybe her bedroom. She moves that typewriter around so much I can't tell for sure. Bobo and

I get our own breakfast, and make some for her too.

We sit in our pajamas at the table, not looking like sister and brother. Our pajamas are identical though. Daddy got us the same ones for Christmas last year.

Bobo's a year younger than me. His face is honey brown and round. Just looking at it you'd think he was four or five. But he's tall and skinny. His pajama legs are too short for him, and mine are still too big for me.

Once at school we had to describe ourselves in ten words. The first word I used was *square*. Everything about me is square. Square face and body. Even my fingernails are square. I don't have charm like Bobo, just common sense, which Mama Dot says isn't so common anymore. My teachers say I'm a decent student if I'd stop dreaming. I lose my book bag so much I don't know if college could ever be right for me. Bobo already knows where he wants to go.

He's also funny and smart, and everybody likes him. He knows what to say to make people feel good. Then there's me.

He's got his face in a comic book. I reach across the table to the box of donuts. I bite into a jelly donut and get a big glop of it on the front of my top.

"Why don't you want to be called Bobo anymore?"

Bobo lowers the comic book and says, "Just call me Robert, okay?"

"Why?"

"Because, 'why.' "

Bobo takes a sip of milk and a bite of sugared donut. He doesn't want to tell me. The more I ask the less likely I am to get an answer, so I don't bug him with it. Sometimes I think he should have been the oldest 'cause I don't get any fun out of bossing him. Usually he smiles and does what you want him to. Now he's leaning his chair back against the stove, looking at me.

I smile at him and finish breakfast, and think about the chores I have to get around to. Bobo's done his already. I heard him sweeping the porch and vacuuming the hall and living room.

We've been doing most of the housework this summer. Mama Dot's been busy with school. She says housework every few days is enough for her. I don't mind, and Bobo doesn't either. Sometimes I catch him standing back admiring what he's just done. I don't let him see me watching though. It'd probably shame him.

4

Bobo chews orange peels while he leans his chair back. That makes me crazy. Who chews orange peels? He knocks the pot holders off the door of the stove, then gets up to pick them off the floor. He looks like he feels sorry for me.

"You want to know why I want to be Robert now?"

I don't say anything. I just look back at him with my mouth full of donut. When he still doesn't tell me I nod my head real fast.

"I hung around the library yesterday. I mean, I just didn't sit there—I read books and looked things up."

"What's that got to do with wanting to be called Robert?"

"It's got everything to do with it."

I start clearing the table. I can see this is going to go on for a while. Bobo can start telling you something in the morning, and the explanations can go on into the night. I put the dishes in the sink and turn around to listen.

Bobo stands by the refrigerator looking at his feet.

"Jolette calls me Robert. She calls me Robert all the time. She was at the library yesterday too."

He leaves the kitchen. I dump milk down the sink. Jolette calls him Robert.

5

TWO

◄O►

Jolette lives next door to my best friend, Viola. Earlier this summer her stepmother, Miss Mary, and two little brothers moved into a house that'd sat empty a few years. Jolette said they were lucky to get it, mold and all, because there's worse things in life to worry about.

When I asked her what she meant she jumped out of the lawn chair, hit Bobo in the arm, then ran through a gap in the fence. That was a week ago.

I guess she's right about worse things, whatever that means to her. She's been around. She's been someplace other than here, I know that. Harvey, Ohio. I mean Harvey's so far out of everything and everybody.

I wouldn't normally be hanging with somebody like Jolette. Number one, she's two years younger than me. Number two, Viola can't stand her, and number three, I don't think the girl has any other friends. I talked to Mama Dot about it. She blew cigarette smoke out the side of her mouth and said something about growing up with charity in my heart.

Jolette makes me think of little kids who follow you down the street wanting to go places with you. She's skinny, about sixty pounds, and always seems to be brushing imaginary strands of hair from her face. I've never seen her without all her hair pulled back though.

Seems like a little wind could blow her in any direction. She makes me a little nervous I guess.

Mama Dot talks about people being judgmental and looks at me when I talk about Jolette. She's always saying Jolette is different. Different isn't good or bad, she says, just different.

I run the water in the sink for the dishes, sticking my arms in to feel the heat. The water feels so good I stand on my tiptoes to put my elbows in. I don't know how long I stand there, but when I look at the clock on the wall the water is cool.

I finish the dishes before Mama Dot brings her typewriter down. Our daddy told Bobo and me that we should take care of her this summer. We would've taken care of her even if he hadn't asked. Daddy wrote us a long letter telling us it was an important time for Mama Dot.

Since the divorce is final, she has to get her degree to get a good job. She needs our help. He says he couldn't really help that much living in Chicago. Like he'd really want to.

Even Mama Dot says he just wants her off his back about money. I think it's cynical but true 'cause the divorce was nasty. She used to scream at Daddy through the phone a lot. I always hated when the phone rang.

By the time I've washed all the dishes the sun is blazing through the kitchen window, and Viola is knocking on the screen door, telling Bobo that the noise he is making throwing the tennis ball against the house is driving her crazy.

She's dressed in combat boots and a long blue

cotton dress. Mama Dot calls Viola an anachronism. I have to look that up. Mama really likes her anyway.

"You home?" Viola yells as she slams the screen door, walks in, and sits at the kitchen table.

"Home and still in my nightclothes," I say.

Viola says, "Want to go down to the river?"

"What's at the river, Viola?"

She eats half a donut from the box and puts the rest back, then looks up and says, "Nothing's at the river—nothing ever has been there—but let's just go."

Viola gets up and paces the floor, her boots clomping. She paces when something is wrong. She goes to the river when something is wrong too.

The river relaxes her, and she never goes there alone. We've been going there since we were in the second grade. We taught ourselves to swim.

Nobody knows that though. We tied ropes around our waists to a big willow tree and pulled each other to the bank. We learned in a couple of weeks. Even though we were eight we knew the danger. Real danger. A couple of kids we'd known had drowned.

I leave Viola in the kitchen and run upstairs to change and check on Mama Dot. She sits in the hall reading, looks up at me, smiles, and tells me not to get in trouble. I put on jeans, a T-shirt, and tennis shoes. Three minutes later Viola and I walk past the projects to the tracks. The river runs alongside.

Viola runs the length of the tracks till we get to our spot by the river. She yells to me to hurry. She flaps her arms and throws her head back as she jumps off the track into the bushes and out of sight before I can get there. I find her sitting under the willow, her boots already off.

We sit quietly. Every now and then garbage floats by us. We watch it go past, or, if it's close enough, we drag it out. Most of it is too far away though. The river stinks but is pretty. The skeleton of an old steel mill looks down on it. Sometimes we throw rocks across to hit the fence that keeps everybody out. Today we just watch the water winding past.

Viola wades out into the shallow part, then turns to face me.

"I was looking out my window last night. I saw Jolette Thomas. She was standing in back of their garage, killing a dog."

THREE

◄○►

Jolette's been jumping rope in front of our house for the last two hours. She started at seven o'clock this morning. Singing. I sit in my bedroom window and watch her skip over a clothesline. Singing and skipping. I watch her till Mama Dot calls me down to breakfast.

Bobo says she's like us—fatherless. Our dad lives in Chicago. He moved there after his and Mama Dot's last big fight. Jolette says even though her dad came home from Vietnam he was still fighting and he didn't seem to be able to find a place to get away from it.

Bobo isn't at the table. Just me and Mama Dot. She highlights lines in her book, and I drink coffee, which she frowns at. Her eyes scrunch up and she almost puts the felt end of the highlighter in her mouth. Probably lost her glasses again or just forgot that she doesn't have them on.

"Art history," she breathes.

"Art history, what?"

She smiles. "Art history doesn't like me. Never has and never will. I have to have it though. A complete education will allow you to get a good job and move into a better neighborhood. It will allow you to expand your circle of experience and grow."

"Sounds like a brochure, Mama."

"It is a brochure."

"You memorized the college brochure?"

"Yeah, strange isn't it? Just wanted to keep it all in mind."

Mama Dot has a photographic memory. She reads something once and she has it.

"All this work so you can curate a museum one day?"

"Curating is really what I want to do. When you and Robert were little I'd take you to the museum in the morning. I thought I could live in that place forever. When I had to go back to work at the factory, I cried."

She sinks into the book she's been reading, while I drink most of my coffee and pull my legs up to my chin. Pot holder patterns dance along the wall and hang off the stove.

Jolette sings outside. Mama Dot looks up from her book and we listen.

"Teddy Bear, Teddy Bear turn around. Teddy Bear, Teddy Bear touch the ground. . . ."

"I used to jump rope to that. Whoa! That was a long time ago, almost thirty years," Mama Dot says. "I'd start from one side of town and skip to the other. All my friends did too. We'd skip all day long until our mothers started calling us in. They had to find us first though."

Mama looks out the kitchen window, squinting again, at the big oak tree leaning against the house.

I hear Bobo out front laughing. I still haven't told him what Viola told me. Can't bring myself to talk about it with him. I don't want to believe it, but I do. Even though she doesn't like Jolette, Viola doesn't lie.

When I got home yesterday from the river I sat and listened to Bobo play his harmonica in the sunflowers in the front yard. Bobo played the harmonica so sweetly I tried to forget all about the dog.

Mama Dot's gone from the table now. No telling how long I've been sitting here. No telling.

FOUR
◄○►

They're saving people over at Holiness Church on Water Street. You can hear it. I'm sitting on top of a mailbox across the street and listening to the saving. Soon people come pouring out after the service looking tired. Old women with their grandbabies on their hips. They wave paper fans across their faces, shiny with sweat.

Mama Dot has the same kind of fans in an old chest. There are pictures of Martin Luther King Jr. and President Kennedy on the front of them. I used to pull them out and use them in plays I made up with Bobo.

The people coming out of the church must have got the Holy Ghost. That's what Mama Dot calls it. She used to go to a church like this one when she was young. Her own mama used to get the Holy Ghost. She'd dance and twirl around so fast she'd pass out. She'd punched out a two-hundred-fifty-pound usher once with the Holy Ghost. She weighed ninety.

I used to wonder if things like that happen at Holiness. Then Jolette told me it did. She said God was loud at Holiness. Not like St. Patrick's that Viola goes to with incense and holy water and God whispering instead of shouting. The Sunday I went with her I could barely hear the priest. He whispered to God.

Nobody at St. Patrick's looked like they'd get up and dance. So I did like them. It was like we were all watching a movie. I didn't know much about church then and guess I still don't.

Everyone at Holiness Church files down the street past deserted storefronts and the municipal parking lots. They're going to the river. I'd watched them baptize people before. I guess if you lived through the dirty water you must have found a secret to eternal salvation.

At the head of the procession is Jolette's stepmother. She wears a gray dress, black high heels, and a hat. Two little boys use what space she's left them. They walk toward the river in their little black suits and red bow ties. When the smallest almost falls she swoops him up and carries him.

I wondered that Jolette could have been related to Miss Mary, but then I found out she was her stepmother.

Miss Mary's whole body eats up the scenery.

I watch from the mailbox until the last person turns the corner, heading for the river. Holiness is just a building now. No life coming out of it. No screams of joy. God must be tired, like the people who filed out of the church a moment ago.

JOLETTE HADN'T been one of the tired people at Holiness, 'cause by the time I get home she's sitting in our yard, under a sunflower, writing in a notebook with her face so close to the pages her nose has ink smears.

"What's up?"

She squints up at me. "Don't you think Ohio's too cold in the winter?"

"Yeah, I guess it's real cold here then."

I guess that's all the answer she needs 'cause she keeps writing.

"Where's Robert?"

"He's looking for stray cats, I think. He said something about being worried about kittens. He's usually worried about one thing or the other."

I leave Jolette alone with her book and walk up the porch steps, thinking that Bobo came out of the divorce better than anybody in the house as far as worrying is concerned. She seemed pretty sure about Bobo and his worries. I like her better for it—knowing Bobo and all.

There's a note in the kitchen from Mama Dot that she's at the library and it's Robert's turn to make dinner.

Even Mama Dot's calling him Robert.

Bobo is what Mama Dot calls "a bright shining light." I guess he's that, nickname or not. I like my brother. It might sound strange, but we've been friends most of our lives.

Bobo calls to me from the front room. He comes in with a cat around his neck. There's scratches on his arms, and his shirt is ripped. But he still has a big old smile on his face.

"I chased this cat for miles. She isn't as friendly as she looks either."

Bobo scratches the cat's head. The orange cat's eyes are almost bigger than her whole head. She lays around Bobo's neck. They both have stupid looks on their faces.

"What's for dinner?"

"That cat if you don't get it out of here," I say, looking at both of them.

Bobo scratches the cat's paws. "This cat is going to be a gift to Jolette. She doesn't know it yet though."

I almost get a lap full of the lemonade I'm drinking. I still haven't said anything to Bobo about the dog and Jolette. Now he's going to give the pet murderer a cat.

"I don't know if you should be giving Jolette a pet, Bo— Robert. I don't think she'd be able to take care of it."

"Yeah, she would. That's why I'm giving her this cat."

I look at Bobo for a long time. I should tell him. Maybe Jolette is nuts. Of course that would make my brother want to be around her even more. Our whole family is like that. Look at Viola. Stray animals and strange people hook us all the time.

19

Anyway maybe Jolette isn't all she seems 'cause something happened a few days ago after Viola told me. "The dog's dead 'cause she killed him."

Now that I've said it I can't look Bobo in the face—so I pay attention to my lemonade like it's going to evaporate in front of me.

"Yeah, I know. . . . I better go wash this cat. I think she has fleas, and Mama Dot will have a fit if she starts getting bit by them."

Talk about dry. I blame Daddy for all of this. Everything has just changed around here, and it just can't be like it was. Everything had solid corners and hard rules when he was with us. Everything's soft and fuzzy now.

The floor is sticky, so I guess I should scrub it. Might as well do it now when I feel like it. It feels good to just work and not think as I scrub the floor till it shines.

FIVE
>◁O▷

Yesterday Jolette kicked the shed door down in her backyard and pulled out a canvas bag full of fake IDs. She poured everything out of the bag and spread all the driver's licenses and state ID cards over the yard. Bobo was so happy he looked at Jolette like he loved her.

I don't know what to think, especially after Jolette told me Miss Mary was the forger—in her other life.

We've been hanging out a lot at Jolette's 'cause me and Bobo love the smell of the house. Jolette's house always has good food-cooking smells. Just about the time the smell disappears it's time for Miss Mary to cook again.

Our house never has good food smells. Maybe if salads could smell. . . . I've even smelled stew cooking at Jolette's house—in the summer, if you can believe it. I sit in the kitchen and watch Miss Mary chop up vegetables.

I thought she'd cut off a finger she was going so fast. It was like art. The vegetables were all chopped so beautifully.

I guess Miss Mary had to put her energy into food when the fake ID business got too hot for her in Columbus. Jolette says that things slacked off after Miss Mary got saved. She didn't stop her business until the pastor got wind of what she was doing and had a session of all-night praying in their living room.

The way Miss Mary told it she couldn't take the risk of losing that much sleep again, so she stopped but kept all her equipment.

I walk around the shed in Jolette's backyard anytime I get the chance. I can't find anything that hints what she did.

I started thinking that maybe it was all a dream of Viola's until I looked up and saw her in her bedroom window. She looked like she was about to faint and fall out the window. She always takes her screen out in the summer so she can sit on the roof. Anyway, Viola does not approve of anything having to do with Jolette.

I tell myself I'm hanging around to watch over Bobo, 'cause the way I see it now, I'm the only one to do it. But the house does smell so good. . . .

Miss Mary says, "Jolette's daddy taught me how to cook greens. I'd never cooked them before because my family was born in North Dakota, where it's really hard to find a soul-food restaurant."

Miss Mary talks and chops. When she isn't doing that she's tasting things from pots and stirring vegetables on the stove. It's like a cooking show, and it makes me feel all warm inside. I wonder if Mama Dot will ever cook. My dad had done it all.

Mostly Mama Dot had handed him things while he yelled at her about smoking over the food.

Miss Mary leans toward Bobo and holds out a spoon for him. He eats the greens like he's coming home from somewhere faraway that's foodless. Then he starts to cry, and all of us except Miss Mary look at our feet.

Miss Mary sings hymns, real soft and sure.

She sings and dishes out bowls of greens and cornbread to the little boys on the floor. She serves Jolette, Bobo, and me last. Bobo's stopped crying, and there's just the food and the steamy kitchen. Miss Mary eats standing up and smiles.

Walking home later, Bobo jumps over all the cracks in the sidewalk. I talk on about how good lunch had been and did he believe that we ate what Daddy used to call Sunday food on a weekday. He acts like he's listening and says, "Uh huh." Halfway home he starts talking.

"Do you think Daddy misses us much?"

"Yeah, I think he does. He calls and writes."

Bobo stops and leans against an old fence. "I don't mean him thinking about us and feeling guilty, then writing. I mean really missing us. So much he can't eat or sleep. So much he can't work or think about anything or anyone but us."

He's making me tired, but I feel bad for him so I just say, "Yeah," and we walk on home.

WE STILL SMELL like Sunday dinner before Sunday dinner became sandwiches, pizza, and

salads. Bobo looks out the window, and I hear
Mama Dot pacing upstairs. I go in the kitchen,
find a piece of paper and a pen, and start the
grocery list for next week. On the top of the list
is greens.

SIX

◄○►

There's a man following us. I've been notic-
ing him for a few days. At first I thought I
was imagining him. Then I started worrying that
it was the cops after me for painting all the smiling
faces on the signs. I saw him while I was grocery
shopping.

Robert was pushing Jolette around in the
shopping cart, and I was looking for them by the
frozen food. There he was. He was the same man
who'd stood across from the park when we'd all
been listening to a concert a couple days ago.

I saw him when he'd bumped into this girl

26

and spilled a grape ice all over her peasant blouse. She'd been pretty mad and had screamed at him. He walked away apologizing and smiling.

Another thing to be on the lookout for. I mean it's not enough that I watch Jolette around that cat that Bobo found for her. I'm staying close to both of them. And now some man's following us around and I think I'm the only one who sees him.

He's tall and has a full beard. He's always wearing sunglasses, so I can never see his face. Most times I feel him before I see him, but when I motion to Robert or Jolette, he's gone. He doesn't scare me yet though, and I wonder why. That's why I haven't told Mama Dot. I'm not scared yet. . . .

Viola tosses her copy of *True Romance* over to me and starts reading *Detective*. I read the article about how this girl had gone out on a blind date and never came home. They'd found one of her platform shoes in a mailbox near the post office in her town.

"I'm never going on a blind date."

Viola screams into the air, "Don't be telling

me the stories before I read them. I hate when you do that. You always do that."

"I don't always do it."

"Yes you do, always."

"When?"

"Remember that story last month about the man found in the deep freeze of that restaurant. I got the magazine just for that story. You waited until my mom was having her daily breakdown to steal it and read it before me."

"I didn't tell you the whole story though."

"No, just the good gory parts."

Jolette and Robert run past. Well, Robert runs past and Jolette skips past with her jump rope.

"How can you let your brother be around her? She's weird."

"Not as much as you would think."

Viola sits up and scratches her leg. She still has on her flowered dress and combat boots. She got her boots from her cousin Earl. Viola has huge feet. I'd been with her the day she dug the boots out of his duffle.

I don't think Earl has ever touched his duffle bag since he got out of the army a couple years ago. Anyway, the boots were heavy, and I wish Viola would stick them in her mouth.

"I think you've lost your mind. What about

that dog? Huh? I mean a person doesn't look out their window and see that every night.''

"Maybe you didn't see it. I mean maybe it was something else. Maybe the dog was already dead."

"Already dead?"

"I don't know. Read your magazine."

We read for a while under the sunflowers. *True Romance* is one of my favorites. Mama Dot calls it trash but won't come right out and tell me not to read it, but she wants to. Just when I think she's going to start in on what I'm reading, I put it away and get on another subject. It works sometimes.

I look over at Viola and watch her eyes get huge. She must be at the part where the shoe's found. I decide to tell her about the man who I think is following us. Viola listens to the whole story and decides I'm missing my dad too much. Just like that.

"Did this man look anything like your dad?"

"No."

"Nothing like him?"

"I said he looked nothing like him. I told you what he looked like. You know my dad. He's short and this dude's tall. I really see this man."

I gotta remember that Viola's mother is a

counselor at a halfway house. She sits around all day long telling kids that their roommates aren't trying to drive them crazy and it can be a problem to clean out your parents' house full of furniture then have a party on the proceeds.

Viola would have died if I'd told her she was acting like her mother.

I get up and go in the house for Hi-C. I'm going to take my time coming back. So I sit and look at a picture of Mama Dot, Daddy, Robert, and me at Nelson's Ledges State Park. Only Daddy's head isn't there. We're all laughing except Daddy, who did, but can't anymore.

Since nobody is around I drink from the can. It's better that way. I figure a few more minutes away from Viola will make me feel better and give her time to quit acting like her mom.

Viola is hiding in back of one of the giant sunflowers as I walk down the steps. She whispers.

"There's a tall man across the street with a beard. I think he's watching this house."

True Detective.

SEVEN

◄○►

When I was younger I thought the Vietnam War was a television program like *Julia* and the *Brady Bunch*. One night I found out the war wasn't just a TV program.

Sometimes we sat in front of the TV with our dinner. Daddy never did though. He'd always have his dinner at the table with his back to the living room and the television.

The night I found out the war was real was when Mama Dot got up from the easy chair, walked over to the TV, stepping over me and Bobo, and turned the set off. The TV never came on again, and Daddy said later that a boy who used to go to school with Mama Dot had died in the war.

Well I'm talking about all this 'cause Jeff Miller is sitting underneath the sunflowers now with me and Viola. I almost had a heart attack when he crossed the street to the yard, but it's okay now.

He's a vet, fatigue jacket and boots just like the ones Viola wears, and he's been following us. He talks about how many kinds of sunflowers there are and drinks Hi-C from a jelly glass.

We're waiting for Jolette. Jeff says that he's been waiting to see her for six years. "I've known her dad forever it seems. We were in the same squad in Nam."

Jeff leans back and looks up to the sky. The sunflowers tower over him, and he doesn't brush off the ants that crawl on him. I wonder if he's hot in all the clothes he's wearing. I mean it is summer and I know he has a sweatshirt on under his jacket, but he looks cool under it all. I hear Jolette and Bobo in the distance.

Jeff asks, "What's up with this town anyway?"

Viola looks up from her magazine. "What do you mean 'what's up?' Nothing is ever up in

Harvey and we should know it 'cause we've lived here all of our lives."

"I mean what's up with all the banners and signs all over town. Is there going to be some kind of town party or something?"

I look at Viola and she looks at me.

"Where have you been that you've forgotten all about the Bicentennial. I mean it's next year. You know, 1976?"

Jeff sits up slowly. "Is it here already? I mean that would make this 1975."

Viola looks up from her magazine. "What year did you think it was anyway?"

"I guess I just didn't think the time was where it is. It's been going slower than I thought, time. I used to feel it whipping by so fast on the road and everything. The Bicentennial, huh? I guess I haven't missed it yet."

Jolette and Bobo step into view and stare at all of us. I guess we look a little strange lying under the sunflowers, and they can't even start to think who Jeff might be. He's kind of young looking but is twenty-five. He looks a little out of place in his fatigues.

Jeff stands up as Jolette comes closer to stare at us.

"You Jolette?"

"Yeah."

"I'm Jeff."

By now Jeff is standing and bowing to her. I've never seen anyone bow before. Viola giggles, and Bobo stands up straighter, then Jolette smiles when Jeff says, "Your dad sent me."

JOLETTE SAYS loving people is dangerous. It can cause you all kinds of problems. It makes you wait a long time for someone to grow up or come around to your way of thinking, 'cause even if you're running out of patience you still have love for the person.

I know what she means.

She sits on the porch with me, Viola, and Bobo and talks about her daddy after Jeff Miller walks on up the street, after promising he'll see her around. He's going to hang around Harvey for a while.

Jolette winds her feet around the pillar on the porch and picks at a scab on her knee and starts telling about her dad and how they ended up in Harvey without him. Viola sits at the far end of the porch and looks off into space, probably not wanting to look too interested.

I know she wants to stand up and ask about the dog, but she looks over at me and fakes reading her romance magazine. All the while Bobo listens and lets the cat walk all over him.

EIGHT
◄○►

I think about Daddy sometimes and get so mad
that he could leave. I remember him sleeping
on the floor by my bed during storms. He'd always
be there when I woke up the next morning.

Sometimes I dream of storms.

JOLETTE and her family—Miss Mary, the two
boys, and her father—lived in Columbus before
they moved to Harvey. They'd lived by a ravine,
and their house was surrounded by trees. In the
fall there were so many leaves in their backyard

the little boys would bury themselves in them for hours. Jolette would watch them. They made her laugh, and she was crazy about them.

Sometimes the little boys hid in the leaves under the trees 'cause they didn't want to be in the house. Jolette says they hid from the father. The father yelled and the little boys hid. If the father yelled in the night the little boys hid under their beds and slept there till the sun came up. I guess he was their storm.

Jolette used to hide, but she stopped.

She'd stopped being afraid the night Miss Mary took the little boys and stayed away from the father for a month. Miss Mary had left Jolette because she was her stepdaughter and figured she should stay with her father. Miss Mary told Jolette she was a good kid but not really hers.

It would be wrong to take her.

Jolette understood and took the money and address Miss Mary handed her. She kissed the little boys and waved to them from behind the trees.

The little boys missed Jolette, so they all came back, but it was still the same after they came back.

It was during a time he was gone that Miss

Mary had found the church. She told Jolette God had been sitting on top of it calling to her.

Jolette said Miss Mary found God on a Saturday morning outside the Big Bear Supermarket. She'd stopped to listen to a man in the parking lot shouting a sermon about love. Jolette and the little boys picked up the fruit that rolled across the parking lot as Miss Mary fell to her knees.

The quiet little boys started wearing suits and bow ties. They got quieter. Miss Mary told them they had to be quiet so God would hear all of their prayers.

Jolette said the father yelled even more as the whole house got quieter. The little boys didn't get to hide under the leaves anymore though. They went to church. Miss Mary would hold her head up and stare into space when the father would start, then she'd put on a hat and march the little boys right out the door.

Jolette could come or stay as she pleased. Sometimes Jolette would go, but mostly she wouldn't. It's not that she didn't like it, she did.

She preferred to jump rope. She'd been doing it since she could walk. She'd jump all through her neighborhood. She was happiest when all she could feel was her feet skipping over the rope. She even jumped rope in the snow. She said it cleared her mind. She took her rope to school 'cause she said her mind was real fuzzy there.

When Miss Mary worried about her jumping so much, the father told Miss Mary that Jolette had been jumping rope since she was a baby in Florida and to leave her alone.

Jolette said she knew Miss Mary worried about it though, so she'd go a couple days without jumping to make her happy. But sometimes at night she'd sneak down in her nightclothes and jump rope up and down the driveway.

On one of these nights the father went away from the house and never came back there. He passed Jolette in the driveway and got in his car. He sat for a minute and watched Jolette jump up and down past him. When she was clear of the car he backed up and drove down the road.

Jolette waved.

The last things Jolette saw in the house before she moved from Columbus were her father's old work boots by the door. She thought about taking them with her just in case. But Miss Mary and the boys were waiting in the van the church had hired to take them all away from Columbus.

When the pastor decided to start a new church, half the congregation left with him. The real estate people in Harvey must have really had to go to work. People just didn't move into Harvey that much anymore. They left Harvey a lot though. For a while you could see U-Hauls everywhere.

Jolette said that Miss Mary took the first place she saw. The house had been empty for years.

Everybody in Harvey knew old Mrs. Chelsea had died in the house. Before she died though, she had been seen for years only in her back wildflower garden, and everybody thought it was kind of sad. She had been nice and had no family to speak of. Mama had known her all her life.

Miss Mary had thanked heaven for shelter and not even asked about the old empty house. She started everybody scrubbing. The little boys helped as much as Jolette did.

Jolette put up curtains and put wildflowers in their bedroom windows. She thought about her father's shoes at the back door in Columbus and wondered where he was and if he'd ever find them. Miss Mary told Jolette that they were never going back to Columbus, but she could if she wanted.

She told her she could even stay and wait, but she left with them.

Jolette came to Harvey and tried to forget about the ravine, the house, and the trees all around it.

Miss Mary told her that her father was a mess. The war had made him that way, and there was nothing any of them could do. When Jolette thought about it, she knew her stepmother was right.

Her father had been unhappy long before he'd even met Miss Mary.

He'd been sad even before Jolette's real mother went away and left them in the big apartment in Florida. One day her father picked her up from her baby-sitter's house in Miami and drove until they were almost to Georgia. They never went back, but he always said he wanted to.

Around the time Jolette had moved to Harvey, I was getting used to Daddy being gone. I didn't wake up in the middle of the night anymore trying to hear his footsteps. The weather had finally gotten hot, and I could kick all the covers off.

I took to listening to the mosquitoes buzzing around the window screens in my room. I'd listen for police sirens and fire engines blowing down the street. I listened to Mama Dot's typewriter. I'd even listen to Bobo and Viola laughing at a late movie on TV. I figured Daddy had been gone long enough for me not to listen for him. It was time I blocked his footsteps out of my mind.

I thought the summer was going to stink. Two weeks before, Mama Dot'd had a tear in her eye when she told me there'd be no money for camp, but it was gone before it fell. That's Mama Dot. She's not the crying kind.

She'd taken me to Ralph's Diner. I remember how the burgers sizzled and smelled so good and how Mama Dot had pushed her coffee around the table and tried to look at anything else but me.

She'd had on her Ohio State T-shirt, which she wore all the time. I guess it was her security blanket. She spilt coffee on her shirt, then shook her head about the mess everything had become. I agreed and ordered more french fries 'cause I knew she loved greasy food and I couldn't think of anything else to do.

In the end we ate five orders of fries and walked home by the tracks. We heard the train coming down the tracks and did what we always did when that happened. We stood and waited beside the ditch until the train was about one hundred feet away, then started screaming as loud as we could. We screamed until it turned the curve in the tracks.

Then we both fell into the ditch, laughing.

NINE
◄O►

We were celebrating Mama Dot's getting on the dean's list when Jeff Miller pulls up in a pickup truck. Jolette and the Doubles are sitting next to him eating red, white, and blue Bomb Pops.

Mama Dot stretches her legs out and stands up. The back of them are webbed from the lawn chair.

"Who's that?"

I say between bites of hot dog, "Jeff. He's a friend of Jolette's."

"Jolette's dad," Bobo says.

"He said he'd been looking for her for a couple of months. Can you believe that? He actually followed us around town looking for her. He watched for a few days before he went up to her. It was spooky before we knew."

Mama Dot stretches and waves to Jolette and the Doubles.

"Why didn't you tell me about someone following you? I don't think anyone tells me anything anymore."

Bobo walks over and leans against her. "We tell you everything," and takes her hand.

He looks like a little boy as he sags against Mama Dot, instead of a twelve-year-old who is now Robert. They both look toward the truck, and Jeff jumps out. His Afro brushes the top of the doorway. He looks at us and smiles, walking toward us.

He bows to Mama Dot. It's the second time I've seen him bow like that.

"Afternoon," he says.

Mama Dot smiles and nods her head at him.

"I'd like to borrow your kids for a while. Just a ride in the country."

Before he can say anymore, Bobo runs to the

45

back of the truck and hops in. He and Jolette talk to each other through the window.

Jeff introduces himself to Mama Dot and says that if she has any reservations she can talk to Miss Mary. Mama Dot puts her hands in the back pocket of her cutoffs and stares at Jeff for a long time. She nods her head at me, then at him. I run for the back of the truck too.

THE HILLS of Kentucky have never been so green. There's a deserted warehouse in the middle of town that we go into to look at Kentucky. I thought looking at the dark hills in the night with the sky lit up behind them was like nothing else I'd ever see. Riding in the back of the pickup through the hills is better. Jeff plays the Funkadelics loud on the eight track, and we all sing through the Kentucky countryside.

Never had a picnic in a pickup before. Jeff pulls the truck over to the side of the road. We perch alongside a scenic view and can see Harvey and more.

Jolette, Bobo, and the Doubles run along the fence that drops into the valley, and all Jeff says to them is be careful. It works. They all move back and find more interesting things farther away from sudden death.

"This is more beautiful than the Grand Canyon," Jeff says.

I move closer.

"When did you see the Grand Canyon?"

"I saw it three months ago. I've probably seen it about fifteen times, but I keep going back. It kind of calls to me."

I don't know what he means, but I nod my head like I do. Then I notice the scar that runs from his ear up to his forehead and try not to stare.

Jolette climbs into the back of the truck and sits next to me. As hot as it is, she's shivering. She looks cold all the time. She picks up a sandwich and talks about her father.

"Last time I saw him it was dark and I don't remember what he was wearing. I keep thinking if I could remember it would make all the difference. It's only been a few months and I'm starting to forget his face."

Jeff stares up at the trees. "When I saw him he was working on a house in Tucson, and I almost had a heart attack 'cause I wasn't expecting him. I mean it was out of the blue. I was

47

walking along picking up cans and there he was, calling to me. I hadn't seen him since he went away on the copter."

Jolette puts her sandwich down.

"Does he miss me?"

Jeff stops staring at the trees and looks at Jolette.

"He talks about you and the boys all the time."

"But does he miss us?"

"He told me about the time you all went to the movies and got kicked out 'cause the boys started dancing in the aisles. He said he told the usher that they weren't bothering anybody so he should just leave them alone, and . . ."

Jolette stares at Jeff.

"But does he miss us?"

Bobo comes alongside the truck with a stick. He hits the tires with it and looks up at Jeff.

"Tell her he misses them. Tell her he's going to come home to them and everything is going to be all right. Tell her they're going to go to the movies again and have Sunday dinner and watch TV together. . . . Tell her."

By the end of it all Jolette is in tears while Bobo leans against the truck, still hitting the tires and looking mad, with me in shock watching him be cruel for the first time in his life.

Jeff stares at the trees again.

"Once when I was at the Canyon I felt myself being drawn toward the edge. There are no fences like that one over there. If you want to drop over there's nothing stopping you. The world is out there for you. Grab it.

"My grandma used to call it the Great Beyond. You don't know why you're going or even if it's good for you. But you know you just have to go. That's exactly what it was like. Exactly."

Jeff jumps out of the pickup and stands by Bobo. They look like they could be related. Jeff calls to the Doubles that it's time to go. He walks over to the view and throws a rock into the valley below.

TEN

◄○►

Mama Dot says Harvey's becoming a place full of just-divorced women and their kids. She says that's the coming thing.

Most of the people I know are divorced—even though Mama Dot says kids can't be. She's just talking when she says that though.

We're as divorced as she is.

Bobo is telling Miss Mary that he doesn't believe in sunsets anymore, and she doesn't know what he means. She's been talking about how this is the year she's going to tell the Doubles about Santa Claus. Bobo sits near the stove, and she moves him when the kitchen starts heating up.

Jolette's forgiven him, and we're all waiting for chocolate chip cookies to come out of the oven. Miss Mary washes her hands and looks at Bobo, who's now digging into the rest of the cookie dough on the table.

"What's this about sunsets, Robert?"

"I said sunsets are like Santa Claus. I don't believe in them anymore."

Miss Mary looks over at me with her eyes real wide. Her face shines. She's the only person I've ever met who wears an apron. Most time she has church clothes on underneath, so I guess that's why. Miss Mary just lets it go 'cause it looks like Bobo doesn't want to talk about it.

Daddy got Bobo believing in sunsets. That was a mistake. When Bobo was about five we all sat on Venice Beach and watched the sunset. I've never seen anything like it. I'll always remember it. Bobo thought it was magic when the sun melted down into the water. Daddy told him it was. He always watched the sun go down, until a few days ago. . . .

Jeff took us all to The Raven drive-in for burgers and fries. Mama Dot went too. Everybody went except Miss Mary, who was in church. She even let the Doubles go, though she said they'd done a few things that needed them to sit through a few hours of sermons.

Mama Dot and Jeff sat in the front of the truck, laughing and talking. We sat in the back of the truck and ate. The sun started to go down and the mosquitoes started coming out. As usual Bobo watched the sunset.

Right before the sun went down a family drove up next to us, the mother and father in the front and the kids in the backseat. Bobo looked at them for a while, then watched the rest of the sun go down.

After the sun finally set he looked at me and said, "It's all a lie. Everything he ever told me about sunsets and magic is a lie. He's not even here and the sun doesn't melt down into the water or the woods. It's not magic; it's just the sun."

Jolette moved over to him and held his hand. The Doubles ate most of his french fries and were quiet until somebody pulled in on the other side of us with a dog. When the women got out of the car to go in the Doubles leaned over and fed the rest of the fries to him.

* * *

MAMA DOT says that Jeff reminds her of her little brother, Jimmy. I hadn't seen Uncle Jimmy in about six years. He's living in Canada somewhere, hiding from the war. We get postcards sometimes. I even got a red and yellow poncho from him once. Mama Dot keeps a picture of them when they were little on the living room table. Both of them are dressed in cowboy hats and have cap pistols.

It's nice to think that Jeff makes Mama Dot less lonely. Most of the time they sit around and talk about things I'm not interested in. I'm never asked to leave though. They sit talking over coffee, a beer or two, and even grape Hi-C.

Over grape Hi-C and talking to Jeff, all of a sudden Mama Dot's like she used to be.

She's here.

And it comes to me that it's been a few months since I've seen her talking to another adult for this long a time. I guess she's just a few years older than Jeff.

When I ask Mama why they have so much to talk about she says, "Shared generation," and tells me to stop chewing on the neck of my T-shirt.

53

When Jeff leaves Mama Dot says, "I think he's lonely."

I say, "Does he really remind you of Uncle Jimmy?"

She pulls at my T-shirt and shakes her head at a wet spot that hasn't dried.

"Yeah, he does. I think that your uncle Jimmy must be lonely in Canada too—I guess that's what I'm really thinking."

"Do you think Daddy is lonely in Chicago?"

It's the first time I've asked Mama Dot about Daddy. I'd gotten a card with flowers all over it from Aunt Janice telling me not to bother her with questions about him. When Mama Dot found out about it she had an hour-long behind-the-door conversation with Aunt Janice long-distance.

She told me to ignore anything her sister had told me 'cause she didn't have a life of her own. She said I could ask her anything at anytime.

I remember nodding and saying okay. I remember saying to myself that Aunt Janice was probably right, so I never asked, until now.

"I think he's as lonely as he allows himself to be."

"What does that mean?"

"I mean, he doesn't have to be lonely, but I think he's being lonely to punish himself."

Mama pulls out a cigarette and looks down. "That's probably something that I shouldn't have told you."

Mama Dot gets up off the porch and walks into the house. She stops, turns around, and holds her hand out to me. I crush her cigarette when I grab her hand.

I CAN'T SLEEP thinking about Daddy being lonely in Chicago and want to call him. It's an hour earlier there. I go into Bobo's room instead and sit on the floor.

There's no moon out tonight, but the street-light pours into his room. By Bobo's old toy box glows a Noah's Ark night-light that he won't give up. I tickle Bobo's feet to wake him up, but he's not asleep.

"Mama Dot thinks Daddy is lonely because he wants to be."

Bobo rustles in the dark. "I don't care if he's lonely. We're alone."

"We've got Mama Dot and all our friends. He doesn't have anybody in Chicago. He's living in an apartment all alone."

Bobo sits up and casts a long shadow from the streetlight.

"We're alone, Doreen. We're alone. Jolette says that we'll get used to it. She says she's always been alone, even with Miss Mary and the Doubles. She says just her caring about her dad makes her alone. She's pretty sure no one else loves him. She's the only one. So forget about him being lonely in Chicago."

I get up off the floor to go back to my room. As I'm closing his door Bobo mumbles into the dark.

"Anyway, he lied about the sunset. We shouldn't care about a man who would lie about something like that. We just shouldn't care."

I fall on my bed and think about a world of people like us. Walking around in the dark, divorced.

ELEVEN

◄O►

We got a box and a telephone call from Daddy today, the hottest day of the year. I spent most of the day on Viola's roof eating taffy and listening to her little brother play "The Purple People Eater" about two hundred times until we heard a crash. Viola was pretty sure her mother had finally hit the record player with a bat.

We watched Jolette from the roof. She sat in her backyard with the cat. Viola just looked at me, then her. Jolette must have just come from church 'cause she was wearing a dress. It didn't look like her. She looked like one of the girls in the perfume ads in a field of flowers. She had a whole bouquet of wildflowers in her hand, and what she did next was like watching a silent movie.

Jolette walked around to the back of their garage and spread the flowers all around. Then she knelt down and prayed. I turned my head 'cause I think that's one of the most private things a person can do. Viola sat and stared though, then climbed back through the hall window instead of her bedroom.

When I looked in on her she was lying on the floor. She didn't seem to want to talk, so I went on home.

Anyway the box that was waiting for me at home made me think of Jolette and the flowers. Daddy had packed the things he sent us in a box that used to hold deodorant.

Flower Fresh.

Mama Dot sat in the easy chair with her purse on her lap. She took deep drags of her cigarette and shook her foot.

"I guess this package is for you and your brother."

I nudged the box with my toe. "I guess so. I'll wait for Bobo though."

We both sat across from each other like we were in a duel. A horn blew outside, and Mama Dot got up and went for the door. She turned and came back to kiss me on the head, then left.

I sat looking at the box like it would explode, but of course it never did, so I had to wait for Bobo.

I'd fallen asleep on the floor beside the box when I heard the front door slam near my head.

Bobo rolled in.

"What's that?"

"Daddy sent it for us. I was waiting for you."

The box could have been a snake the way he looked at it. I went to the kitchen and got a knife. We held our breath. Maybe we expected Daddy himself to pop out, but it was only clothes and notebook paper and pencils for school.

We dug through everything quietly. It all probably fit. We'd turned the box upside down when a manila envelope slipped out. I pulled it out from under the couch while Bobo made footballs from one of the paper pads. I took out a color print of the Chicago skyline at sunset. Bobo looked up, stared at it for a minute, then left the room.

* * *

THE MOSQUITOES were out under the streetlights and Mama Dot wasn't home yet when Daddy called.

"How'd you and your brother like what I sent you?"

"We like everything fine, Daddy."

"Does everything fit?"

"It fits fine, Daddy."

"How's the weather? I hear it's real hot there."

"It is."

"How you doin', baby?"

"Daddy?"

"Yeah?"

"When are you coming home?"

When he didn't answer for a minute I heard the phone upstairs click, then Bobo walking down the stairs slowly. He walked over to the coffee table and tore the Chicago sunset up before Daddy could speak again. When I tried to give him the phone he shook his head.

"Never again," was all he said before he went to sit out on the porch with the mosquitoes and the streetlights.

As hot as it was I could smell fall in the air.

TWELVE
—◀○▶—

I made another raid on the Bicentennial signs
last night. Instead of smiling faces I put full
moons and big *D*s on all of them.

I lay down by the old courthouse with my
paintbrush and bucket of fuchsia paint. The
moon shone so bright that it almost felt like mid-
day under the courthouse lights. I felt so good.
I sure didn't feel like a criminal.

JOLETTE SAYS that in Columbus they had a neighbor who whispered. Never raised his voice above

one. He was in the war too, and without ever having been hit by a bullet or anything he lost most of his voice and no doctor could ever get it back for him. Jolette said she'd always wondered if he'd have gone back to Vietnam if he could have found what he lost there.

It bothered her. She'd hang around the man's house and stare at him if he was in the yard. If he wasn't in his yard seeing to his garden she'd make a commotion to get him out of the house. When I asked her what she'd intended to have happen by bothering him, she said she was trying to help him find his voice.

She thought if he could get mad enough at her he'd start yelling. She'd told her dad what she was doing and he'd told her to stop. He figured if the neighbor started yelling he might not ever stop, and that had been that.

She figured between big slurping noises of her Coke that Robert would start talking to our dad again.

"I mean it's not like Bobo's been in a war or anything. Worse things happen to people and they never stop talking to people."

"It's not his way though, the not talking I mean."

Jolette blows bubbles in her Coke and shrugs her shoulders. I finally do too.

I SPENT most of last night sitting in my window trying to figure out what I was going to do when I left school. When Daddy was here it was all set, but him leaving and all changed that.

In a blink all I thought would be wasn't. And all that time, I had taken everything for granted like most people.

Got this picture of me and Daddy in the park. I must have been about six months old with an Ohio State sweatshirt covering my body, and Daddy just laughing his head off. I guess he didn't know just how funny it all really was.

I knew it the first day of kindergarten. The first day. Formal education and me would not get along.

School scared me. There were too many colors and stations to go to. I never understood the time-out chair, which was unfortunate, since I spent most of my time in it. Daddy spent a lot of time at my school. Mama Dot got fed up sometimes, so they had started taking turns.

I am not like I was before. I sit quietly now,

and if you were a stranger just coming into the classroom you'd think, YES, she knows what's going on. I can see it in her face. If you thought like that stranger you'd always be wrong. Always. And it's only the third day of school.

JOLETTE SITS in our living room a lot. She squints at the newspaper and taps her feet when she likes the music that comes on the radio. Bobo does the same. I watch 'cause I don't read the paper and never know what's going on. I never listen to the radio because they clean up all the songs. They cut the heart out of music, so I go without.

I like watching my brother though. Always have. I used to spend hours staring at him in his crib. I could just stay there all day. His nap times were quiet times for Mama 'cause I'd be right there on my bed watching.

Been watching Bobo all his life. It comforts me to see him sitting in the big green chair reading the *Sunday Times* he picks up from the News and Photo Shoppe. He reads it slowly so it will last all week.

* * *

I JUMP UP to answer the phone while Bobo and Jolette giggle at something that's being said on the radio. I'd been staring into space for about an hour. I could hear Mama Dot's typewriter in some other part of the house.

I talked to Daddy for half an hour. I kept asking him questions about Chicago and his job. I wanted to tire him out. Maybe he'd forget about his son this time. The son who was not about to talk to him. After I'd talked about every stupid thing I could think of, a long sigh came through the phone. "I guess I don't need to talk to your brother today, huh?"

"Not today," I whispered. Daddy hung up and Bobo kept laughing at the radio as the DJ told a story about a man who came home from work to find his house gone.

THIRTEEN
◄○►

Jeff Miller got a job at the new water plant that he says is going to help him pay for his trip to Maine. There's an old war buddy of his who is paralyzed there he wants to stay with for a while. He also hauls away stuff to the dump for people. He's hauling stuff for Miss Mary now. She directs everybody as we clean out the shed.

I know Jeff is doing this for free. I'd heard him and Miss Mary arguing about it. She wanted to pay, and he wouldn't take the money.

Mama Dot thinks Jeff shows up at places to take care of his old platoon members' families if they need it, like some guardian angel. I like thinking that angels can have Afros.

I mean there's a whole lotta kids running around Harvey needing guardian angels. There's a whole lotta us missing something. I've been running around all summer missing something.

BOBO AND JOLETTE are in the shed now. The Doubles run around the yard in circles not helping.

Jolette drags out a dirty crate and pulls it to the side to look in it.

"It's old seventy-eight-speed records."

Bobo kneels down and uncovers more of them. "We could always take them down to the record shop to see if they'd want 'em I guess."

They drag the crate to the side and come back to finish in the shed. I'm hoping there's more bags of fake IDs in the shed. I told Viola about them the other day, and she was interested. Maybe that's why she was pulling out an old carpet now. She's changed toward Jolette since that day on the roof, and we didn't even talk about it.

* * *

ALL OF US sit on the back of Miss Mary's porch and drink Kool-Aid and eat ham sandwiches. Jeff tells us about the jungle and Jolette's father, Frank.

"He liked the way Vietnam looked. He said it reminded him of the best parts of Florida."

Viola propped her feet on the steps.

"He liked Vietnam?"

"I didn't say he liked it, I said he liked the way it looked. He said he used to sing hymns before he went out into the jungle."

Miss Mary seemed surprised about it all but didn't mind Jeff talking about the man who left her. There'd probably never be a divorce. She accepted that her husband had a life wherever he was.

Jolette listens and smiles at the things that Jeff says about her dad. Bobo frowns through it all. He's out with fathers, and I don't know if that'll change.

VIOLA SAYS that she thought she was having a dream last night. She figures it wasn't a dream 'cause she heard her brother snoring in it. She says she saw Jolette and Bobo near the shed, dancing. The light from the shed glowed around them. She says they were slow dancing to some old tinny, scratchy music.

Bobo was stepping on Jolette's feet a lot and they were giggling, but the really weird part was that the cat seemed to be dancing to the music too. She stood on her hind legs, pawing at something Viola couldn't see; and on they danced. Before she can tell me any more the study hall teacher tells us to shut up or we'll have to write until the period is over.

Bobo PULLS out an album. "It's called *Songs of Faith and Redemption*. We found it in the crate in the shed. Jolette said she was going to teach me to slow dance."

"Why do you want to slow dance?"

Bobo looks uncomfortable. "We have dances this year, the seventh grade I mean. I don't want to look too stupid."

While I had him talking I ask, "When are you going to start talking to Daddy again? He misses you. He calls and knows you're here."

Bobo gets up from the kitchen table and walks out the back door. Mama Dot stands in the doorway letting an unfiltered cigarette burn her fingers.

I MET Viola at Ralph's Diner. She's sitting in the corner booth doing her homework and eating onion rings and a fish sandwich. I slide into the booth beside her and start eating her onion rings.

"Want to go swimming?"

She says, "Did you know they're dumping things in the river. It smells real bad. My dad says Harvey's going to hell. But I guess that's because the steel mill shut down."

"Is he still screaming around the house?"

"No, that's my mom." Viola laughs and shuts her book.

"We don't have to swim. We can just walk down the tracks and look at the water. The smell won't be so bad then."

Hardly any traffic passed us on the way to the tracks. We didn't have to worry about the traffic anymore from the three-thirty shift change, and only half the number of trains now ran on the tracks. We ran and danced along the tracks, stopping only to look in the river for a minute.

FOURTEEN
◄O►

Three things happened in October.

First, Viola and her family moved. Second, some archaeology students from the college found a cemetery underneath the junior high, which raised hopes of no school for hundreds. Those hopes crashed when they had to dig up only the teachers' parking lot and bring in a priest.

The rumors still flew about people seeing blood run down the walls by the third-floor girls' bathroom though.

The third thing was my brother, Robert, stopped talking, completely.

October's almost over and it's a good thing 'cause I don't think I can take too much more of it. I used to like fall's red and gold leaves blowing around. Robert liked it too. But now I can't stand to think of me standing beside him in all the crackling leaves.

THE CAT slept at the foot of my bed last night and I had wild animal dreams. They'd all escaped from the zoo and were sitting in our kitchen. Mama Dot just sat there typing and drinking coffee.

I need more sleep and have been getting it by sleeping in class. I spend a lot of time in detention, which is okay 'cause I don't have much to do after school with Viola gone.

The day after Viola's family moved to Connecticut, Mama Dot took me shopping and then to Ralph's Diner. We sat at the counter and watched the fryer steam. Viola and I had done this most of the summer. We'd hang out, then head to Ralph's to watch people.

"Your dad and I had our wedding dinner here and I spilled ketchup all over my suit."

I turned to look at Mama Dot.

"You wore a suit?"

She smiled.

"I'll unpack it for you sometime. I got married in a hurry, before either of us changed our minds. I tripped in the judge's chambers and twisted my ankle. My aunt had warned me marriage would probably kill me."

"Your wedding day sounds pretty bad to me."

Mama Dot then talks about how much fun she and Daddy did have, and I start wondering how people who enjoyed each other so much could ever stand being away from each other. I knew the answer though. They just go, like Jeff says, to the Great Beyond.

ROBERT SITS on the porch, occasionally brushing leaves off his homework paper and scratching the cat's head. It's now the tenth day of the quiet. I don't think he'll be talking anytime soon.

The third day Mama Dot got worried, then mad, when the counselor at school told her to ignore him. So she did the opposite and did everything but shake noise out of him. When that didn't work she bought a lot of junk food and stayed up late at night eating it.

73

About two days ago I'd had it and just gave up trying to get a sound out of him. Since he will shrug and shake or nod his head, it's not too bad. I just have to remember to ask yes and no questions.

It's not as bad as it sounds after a while—Robert not talking. Since we live with it. Not so for Daddy though. He's sending money to get Robert "help." I don't know if help will do it, so I've gotten used to answering the phone when he's around and speaking for him when he's asked something by someone who doesn't know.

I step over Robert and hop off the porch to sit under the skeleton of our sunflowers in the front yard. When I was little I thought the big flowers could protect you from the rain. Every time it sprinkled I'd run into the front yard and get under one. Every time. I watched my brother with his face in his book. After turning the page he looks up at me and smiles, and I feel a drop of rain on my face.

FIFTEEN

I should talk about Viola leaving. I should talk about it, but I'm having a hard time.

Everybody's going when I really need them to just stay put. Everyone leaves.

Viola knew a long time ago that she was leaving Harvey. She says she eavesdropped on her parents way back in May and had been miserable about it ever since. It was her worst bad habit I think, eavesdropping.

In the end you always hear something that you really don't want to.

* * *

THAT LAST WEEK we walked home from school every day together. We hung around Ralph's and almost got kicked out for getting ketchup on the walls.

Viola had changed her boots for Earth shoes she'd painted with peace signs. I liked the way they looked. She took them off as we were walking by the pawnshop and handed them to me.

In the park she said, "I hear it's real pretty around New Haven."

I say, "Yeah, I heard that."

Viola starts over to a swing and jumps on it. For the next thirty minutes she swings as high and fast as she can. I squat down by the sliding board and watch her fly in the air.

She slows down after a while and finally just sits.

We watch some little kids rolling past us on their Big Wheels. They'd speed up and spin out over by the gravel in the parking lot. Each time they did it was like the first time. I've never seen such happiness over something like that.

Me and Viola smile at each other.

Viola flexes her feet.

"Do you hate your father?"

"I did hate him—I mean, after he first left.

I couldn't even stand to think about him most times."

Viola slides off the swing and comes over to sit by me.

"How about now?"

"I don't know about now."

But I really do. I spent the whole summer trying not to think about where my whole family had gone. Mama Dot had been there but kind of not there most of the time. Robert was definitely there. It felt good to know he was. But now, he was kind of gone too.

"So do you think your brother will start talking again?"

I look over at the kids laughing their heads off on their Big Wheels. Robert used to laugh like that.

I say, "I don't know."

Viola gets up out of the swing and walks toward the street. I stand up and follow.

THE NIGHT before Viola left she stayed at my house. It was a warm Friday night, so Mama Dot let us sleep out in the backyard.

All night long Robert played servant and

brought us anything we wanted out of the refrigerator. I think we ate two cans of Cheez Whiz
and a box and a half of crackers. We spilled a
whole can of Hi-C in my sleeping bag and the
tent smelled like a huge grape Popsicle.

It was a great night.

At three in the morning me and Viola
exchanged friendship rings. We sat around a
flashlight we'd stood straight up and looked like
ghouls.

I said, "Friends forever."

Then we spit on the ground, put the rings
on, and toasted each other with cans of Mountain
Dew. We laughed about nothing much for the
rest of the night. It was easier that way. Much
easier.

BOBO AND Jolette stood beside me as the U-Haul
pulled away from Viola's house. Viola and her
mom drove away behind it in their car.

She rolled down the window and yelled—
hanging halfway out. I saw her mom trying to
pull her into the car, but it didn't make much
difference. Viola waved and screamed all the way
through Harvey.

* * *

Mama Dot sits next to me on the back steps and offers me a drink of her coffee. It's nice and sweet. I think she made it special for me.

"So what's happening?"

I catch a red leaf from the maple tree and press it to my face. I love the smell of fall leaves.

I say, "Viola's gone now."

"I know. What are you going to do next?"

I think of something smart-mouthed to say until I remember that she's just shared her coffee with me. All I want to do now is cry, but I don't tell her that. One child mute and the other one blubbering would just about make her year complete I guess.

"I want for nobody else to go away. I want everybody to stay put."

I walk away from Mama Dot and go lean against the maple tree. That tree has been here forever and I want people to do like it does. Stay.

Mama Dot comes over and pulls me to the ground.

"I'm still here, baby. I'm not going anywhere."

I give up being mad and lean my head against

her peasant blouse. She smells like cigarettes, coffee, and mint gum. Now that she's done with her schoolwork she's more real for me.

"Bad summer, baby?"

I think a minute and say, "Hot summer, sad summer, an everybody-leaving-me-and-going-away summer. I missed you."

Mama Dot closes her eyes.

"The day I found out I was pregnant with you was the summer solstice. It made sense that the happiest day of my life should be the longest day of the year. It made everything that I had always feared about having a baby seem right. I was only a few years older than you are now, but I suddenly knew everything would be all right and you'd be with me forever. It didn't matter where you went or how long you stayed away. You can't tear this kind of love away. Love and faith, that's all it is."

Mama Dot smiles and changes her mind about lighting her cigarette. She moves me a little until we're lying flat on our backs looking up through the maple. We stay there quiet, letting the leaves fall on us.

SIXTEEN
◄○►

Harvey's fire department is volunteer, and I always wondered how that could be. Did it mean you'd never know if anyone would show up to fight a fire if no one volunteered that day? I worried about it all the time when I was younger. The trucks flash by our house a couple times an hour it seems. I'm used to them now and don't worry as much.

Bobo and I used to bet each other which direction the trucks would go. He'd always yell "the projects" before I did and win. He still sits in the window and watches the volunteers chase fires but can't take part in the game any-more.

Jolette skips up to the porch with her jump rope, hood on her head as usual.

"Is he here?"

I point up.

"What's he doing?"

Bobo's face is pressed to the bedroom window when we step off the porch to watch him. He sees us and smiles through the glass. Jolette waves him down.

He sort of skips when he walks. He's always done it. I always thought it was the talking rhythm that made him do it. Nothing's changed about him except the talking.

BEFORE he stopped talking Robert told me that he'd been hangin' out by the park in the begin-ning of the summer. He'd watched little kids playing in sandboxes and women pushing their babies in strollers. Every day started looking like the one before.

It had been a long time since he'd been in Harvey in the summer. Everybody he usually hung out with was at camp or on vacation with their families. Even though there were always things to do at the house, he'd left it a lot to me. He felt bad about that.

He'd wake when he heard Mama Dot's typewriter, and it would be the start of a new day that he didn't know what to do with. He missed Daddy. His heart hurt him.

Then, on a Wednesday, a couple weeks into June, he started wandering all over, by the tracks and past all the empty factory buildings. A couple of times he'd tried to look in one of them, but they had dogs patrolling all the fenced-in parts.

Harvey was so old. It looked old, but Robert always figured that was because it was tired and poor with the mills gone. The mills had made it look dirty. He said he didn't remember the smells coming from them. Everyone who did remember said it was pretty bad though.

He met Jolette while he was walking around tired old Harvey.

JOLETTE SAT in the back of Holiness Baptist five times a week. She was really trying to give up her jump rope habit. Miss Mary had told her that she, not knowing Harvey, could jump into a bad neighborhood and why didn't she just be a nice girl this summer and sit still.

The church had once been a store. There was still a freezer on the far side of the sanctuary. Mostly Jolette looked at the freezer and kept the little boys quiet. She took them to the bathroom when they needed to go and waved a paper fan over them when it got too hot. They had fans with Martin Luther King Jr. on one side and a funeral home ad on the other. Church usually lasted five hours.

Miss Mary sat in the front on one of the folding chairs. Jolette had been there when the church had bought them at auction. HAWKINS STATE MENTAL INSTITUTION was painted over on the back of them. God was there too, Jolette thought, when she ran her hand over the back of the chair.

When they weren't in church Jolette took care of her brothers, since Miss Mary had a job in the church restaurant that had just opened. The boys were easy to care for because they never thought about leaving the yard and exploring. They stayed put, just like Jolette had been asked.

One day, while the little boys piled rocks up in the front yard of the house on Cater Street, Jolette started jumping rope. She skipped down the gravel driveway and down the sidewalk. She didn't know the little boys had followed her until the youngest asked when they'd eat lunch. She was a mile from their house. She'd jumped all the way to one of the old mills.

They all watched as a boy tried to climb over the mill fence but changed his mind when three dogs came out of nowhere. The boy jumped down from the fence and waved to them. The little boys looked up at her, then waved back. She took them home for peanut butter and jelly sandwiches.

ROBERT HAD SAID he used to pass the old house on the way to school but never believed it was haunted like some said.

He'd never seen old Mrs. Chelsea, the previous owner. Suddenly though he thought the house might be haunted. There were curtains in the window and three kids in the yard. The little boys waved to him and looked up at an older girl wearing glasses. He'd seen this all before, and for a second thought he was going crazy, then I remembered the mill.

It was so spooky; the little boys looking up at

the girl and waving, again. Ghosts. The little boys sat down after a while and piled rocks. The girl in the glasses looked for a few more seconds then walked into the house.

He'd told Mama Dot that some people were living in the house next to Viola. She looked up from her book and said, "Oh really. It's about time."

Mama Dot went back to her reading. He told her the people had at least three kids and that he thought they were ghosts at first. Mama Dot said that would make the summer fun.

The next day they were walking all over Harvey together, telling each other everything that they thought the other person should know about them—Robert walking with a jumping skip in his step, telling his new friend all about his life.

They probably looked the same as they did today going down the sidewalk. Jolette's head is bobbing and she's using her hands as she talks. When they cross the street and turn the corner, a fire truck screams past them and Robert doesn't even look up.

SEVENTEEN
◄O►

My daddy's shorter than I remember. Seems like in early spring of this year I could sit on his lap.

He smells of Old Spice and Afro Sheen, standing beside the couch in the living room like he just got up from a nap. I don't think I let him go for an hour. The smell of Old Spice has to stay with me forever even if he doesn't.

MISS MARY says she has been getting up and praying for Robert in the middle of the night. I feel guilty 'cause I have to say not too much will wake me up when the nights start to get cool.

Jeff says he thinks about Robert a lot but he doesn't pray about it. He doesn't think it's a praying thing, Robert not talking. He thinks it's just something that's going to take time, like my missing Viola.

Miss Mary will say that her praying got our daddy here, and Jeff will say it was just a matter of time. It doesn't matter.

WE ALL SIT around the kitchen table eating salad and pepperoni pizza. My mood ring has turned dark, but my math teacher said it's caused by body temperature not feelings.

Daddy clears his throat. "Everybody looks good."

Mama Dot has her best face on as she looks at Robert, who hasn't looked at Daddy since he came home from school to find him sitting on the couch. He goes upstairs to his room and closes the door.

I'd heard Mama Dot telling Aunt Janice that the psychologist said that we weren't to confront Robert about his not talking. I grab Daddy's hand when he looks like he's going after Robert.

It's a strange feeling stopping my dad from doing something. He just grabs my hand back and sits back down.

I ask, "Did you fly?"

Daddy smiles real slowly.

"Yes I did. I'd have preferred the bus, on the ground." He looks over where Robert had been sitting and says, "But I had to get here quick."

The rest of dinner is quiet. Robert comes back down to us. We listen to the wind blowing the leaves through the backyard. Daddy listens and eats like it's the most natural thing in the world. You'd think he'd never left Harvey, Ohio. I was hoping he was remembering all the good things.

When we finish he and Mama Dot start clearing the table and washing dishes. Robert and me leave it to them and go to the living room.

Robert sits next to me on the couch and yawns. When the cat scratches at the screen he gets up and lets her in, then takes her upstairs. Mama Dot and Daddy whisper in the kitchen while *Songs of Faith and Redemption* drifts down the stairs from my brother's room.

EIGHTEEN

◄○►

Jeff picked Robert up after school today. He offers me and Jolette a ride with them to the dump, but we say we want to walk.

"Jeff's leaving in a little while," Jolette says. We cross Cater Street.

"He's got enough money to get to Maine now, I guess."

She winds her jump rope around her shoulders.

"I'm going to miss him, him bringing news of my dad and all."

"Do you think your dad will ever come back? I mean, he cared enough to send Jeff."

Jolette drops her books on the curb of the street, then covers her head up with her hood.

"I don't think he's ever coming back, but if he does and we're not here, tell him where we went, okay?"

I thought that was a strange thing to say.

"What makes you think I'll be here and you won't?"

"Some people stay and some people go. That's just the way it is."

Viola sends me a tape in the mail. She doesn't like to write. She says New Haven is nice. She takes walks around Yale all the time and it looks just like those eastern colleges on TV. The Funka-delics' music plays in the background.

Her dad's job is working out, and her mom has more than enough job offers to work in half-way houses. Viola says she's given up her boots 'cause she gets too much hassle from people.

She thought the East Coast would be a little cooler than Harvey, but she's found a drugstore up the street that sells *True Romance* and *Detective* magazines. She says she'll send me her old ones, and 'bye for now.

I decide to play the tape for Daddy 'cause he always liked Viola.

W HEN I woke up this morning Robert was sleeping on the couch with Daddy. It got real cold overnight and felt like snow. Mama Dot is still in bed; she has late classes.

I tiptoe through the living room and watch Daddy and Robert sleep from the kitchen. Robert is still wordless, but last night I found him in the kitchen taping the picture of the sunset together. Anything Daddy may have said to him hasn't been told to me. I put on the percolator. For the first time in a long time I listen to the radio.

I hear Daddy rustling around the living room. His foot steps are heavy, different from Robert's. I watch him pull a sweater over his pajamas and come into the kitchen.

"Mmm, coffee. When did you learn to make coffee?"

"This summer. For Mama Dot. You told us to take care of her."

Daddy sips the coffee that I hand him and puts two teaspoons of sugar in it.

"Sometimes when I sit in my apartment I can

almost hear you and your brother running up and down the stairs. I get up to yell for both of you to stop, then realize it's the neighbor's kids running in the hallway."

Daddy keeps sipping his coffee and looks out the kitchen window. I sit and drink my coffee.

"Growing up pretty fast aren't you, baby?"

"No. Just growing up."

He gets up and stands by the doorway. "Doreen. You know I didn't come to stay, don't you?"

I didn't know that, but I say I do. It's the only thing I feel I can say.

"I'd love to have it the way it was a long time ago. It can't be that way anymore though. Mom and me."

"I know. It's over and it's nobody's fault. I know it."

I can't help it. I cry. Daddy doesn't smell like Old Spice this morning. He smells of soapy wool, and he seems taller to me this time with his arms around me.

JEFF STOPS BY before we go to school to say good-bye in a red, white, and blue shirt and his fatigues.

He stands in the door, too shy with Daddy in the house to come in. He gives Daddy a handshake and hugs me and Robert, then slowly walks in and sits.

Mama and him talk for a while about nothing in particular and he gets up to leave.

I follow him to the door.

"Can you stop in New Haven and see about Viola for me?"

He says, "Oh yeah, kid. I'll stop and check her out for you. You got her address?"

I run upstairs to get her address and see Jolette sitting on the hood of his truck through my bedroom window. I hand the address to Jeff a few seconds later and he gives me and Mama Dot one last hug and nods to Robert.

A few minutes later we hear his truck pull off, and I go to the window to see Jolette walking in the opposite direction.

I CAN'T KEEP my mind on anything at school and get detention for not having my homework. When I get home there are three suitcases sitting near the doorway. I stand in the door letting all the cold air inside the house.

I thought Daddy had taken everything with him the first time, but when Robert comes downstairs with his coat on I don't even feel the cold air.

Some will stay and some will go.

Robert walks over and sits on one of his suitcases.

"They got me out of school early today," are the first words he's uttered in more than a month, but it seems real natural.

"You got your voice back, huh?"

Aunt Janice once told my dad that me and Robert would grow up with dry senses of humor and always make a lot of understatements. I remember I looked up *understatement* in the dictionary and figured Aunt Janice would probably be right.

Mama Dot and Daddy are dry and understated. I knew I was meant to accept Robert leaving without too much talk.

I don't talk. I sit with Robert on his suitcase and listen to Mama Dot and Daddy upstairs talking. I hear Mama Dot say, ". . . just until he's better."

Robert moves closer to me and holds my hand.

He leans over and whispers to me, "I made a deal, Doreen."

He walks to the stairs and looks up them.

"Jolette once told me that she'd made a deal with herself about her dad. She said she told herself he'd come back if she jumped one million times with her rope. She didn't have to do it all at one time or anything. She decided if she did that he'd come back. She's only up to about eighty thousand jumps so far."

I scratch at the tweed on the suitcase and think about the deal and how it works. Robert isn't smiling like somebody who's won though.

I shake my head. "All that time—"

"I made a deal and that's all that matters. I wasn't lying or anything. I didn't want to talk. I had to stop. I had to make my deal. I couldn't very well jump rope around Harvey."

I look at Robert and know I'll never figure out people's hearts.

NINETEEN
◄○►

They called school off this morning because of an early snowstorm. Robert missed it, leaving last night. I woke up to a yard full of snow angels and Jolette's sitting on the front porch.

Mama Dot hasn't noticed her or the angels.

I open the door for her to come in and have some cocoa or something.

"You look like a snowman," I say.

Jolette shakes the snow off and grins. Her glasses are fogged up, and the hood on her coat had frozen and stands straight up on her head.

"You mean I look like a snow angel. You know there's no school?"

"This won't happen too much, believe me. I've lived here all my life, and they don't call school off much 'cause everybody lives in town."

Mama Dot comes to the door and takes Jolette's coat and puts it on the radiator, then follows us into the kitchen.

"You girls want me to make you some pancakes or eggs?"

I don't remember Mama Dot ever making pancakes.

"I'm staying home today from school even though they haven't canceled me. I'm ready to cook."

We tell her we'll eat anything, and she takes us at our word and cooks a five-course breakfast. After we've stuffed our faces Mama Dot sips decaf and talks about art and maybe me and her going to New York this summer to the museums.

Jolette said she'd gone to a gallery in Columbus once and had stared at a painting for two hours of a woman walking down a road.

Mama Dot says, "Isn't it incredible when art is hypnotic?"

She stands, kisses me on the head for a long time, then goes upstairs.

Jolette smiles and nods.

* * *

JOLETTE AND ME walk down to the tracks. She talks about Robert.

"I guess he's going to be happy. He stopped by my house on the way to the airport."

"I guess so."

"If he never lives with you again will it be the saddest thing that's happened to you, Doreen?"

"The saddest thing was my dad going in the first place," I say as I make big footprints in the snow.

Jolette picks a rock up and throws it across the tracks and hits the fence of the old steel mill. She skips along the tracks like she has a jump rope. I have to run to catch up to her.

She blows warm air out of her mouth steadily like it's something she just found out she could do. "Can I tell you something, Doreen?"

"I guess so."

"I don't think I can ever be as sad as I was early this summer. I thought my mom dying and my dad leaving would be it. I know I miss them. I know I was sad, but it was something I couldn't do anything about."

It starts snowing again. The mills have never looked so pretty. It's so quiet we hear the river.

99

Jolette walks along ahead of me, then turns to face me.

"I had to kill a dog this summer. He was dying already. I found him down the street a couple minutes after he'd been hit by a car. I couldn't let him suffer. I've been worrying about it."

"It's all right. It's going to be all right."

She says, "I just wanted my dad to come, tell me what to do—take the dog to a vet—help me. . . ."

Tears start freezing up on her face. I put my arm around her and we walk down the tracks and hear only the river running by.

I feel like crying too 'cause I know what she means.

TWENTY

Our house is quiet in the snow. But that wouldn't really make any difference anyway. The snow I mean.

Mama Dot has decided to paint all the walls in the house. She found my fuchsia paint and thought the living room would look great in it.

I had sort of given up being the mad painter of Harvey. They just kept scraping the signs and repainting all the Bicentennial slogans anyway. It's hard to be ahead of your time. Sometimes it's so hard you just have to hang loose—until the world catches up to you.

I have decided my sign- and billboard-painting days are over.

I think about it and I kind of think I was trying to say something but none of it came out like I wanted it to. I should have been painting my dad's face up there on those signs.

I wanted him in Harvey.

Robert calls tonight and says Chicago has good pizza and he likes the sound the wind makes when it goes around buildings.

Robert says before he went away he walked all over Harvey. He climbed every hill in town, always seeing Kentucky in the distance, and thinking of Jeff and the summer.

He found some broken albums on a hill over-looking the old steel mill. He says they were all stacked in a pile and had probably been there for a long time. He says he couldn't read all the titles, but one he could see read *Songs of Faith and Redemption....*

For a minute he stood there, then looked over his shoulder expecting to see Jolette laughing at the joke. He thought maybe the records were a sign for him to stay. But it came to him that the hill was just a dumping ground with the mill on one side and the river on the other.

Then he talks to Mama Dot for a while and tells her to remind me to feed the cat when she comes over to visit us, and not to miss him 'cause he's just fine.

When I look out the window the snow angels have just about disappeared, and I hope the wind that's blown them away will find its way to my brother, but not chill me and my mother too much.